CHICK 'n' PUG
Meet
THE DUDE

For my pack: P, M, L, H, and D.

Home is where you are.

First published in the United States of America in June 2013
by Bloomsbury Children's Books
www.bloomsbury.com

For information about permission to reproduce selections from this book, write to
Permissions, Bloomsbury Children's Books, 175 Fifth Avenue, New York, New York 10010
Bloomsbury books may be purchased for business or promotional use. For information on bulk purchases
please contact Macmillan Corporate and Premium Sales Department at specialmarkets@macmillan.com

Library of Congress Cataloging-in-Publication Data
Sattler, Jennifer Gordon.
Chick 'n' Pug meet the Dude / written and illustrated by Jennifer Sattler. – 1st U.S. ed.
p.   cm.
Summary: While Pug continues relaxing, Chick goes after the Dude, an enormous dog that stole their favorite toy during their nap.
ISBN 978-1-59990-600-3 (hardcover) • ISBN 978-1-59990-760-4 (reinforced)
[1. Roosters–Fiction. 2. Pug–Fiction. 3. Dogs–Fiction. 4. Adventure and adventurers–Fiction.] I. Title. II. Title: Chick and Pug meet the Dude.
PZ7.S24935Chm 2013   [E]–dc23   2012030502

Art created with acrylics and colored pencil
Typeset in Cafeteria and Draftsman Casual
Book design by Nicole Gastonguay

Printed in China by C&C Offset Printing Co., Ltd., Shenzhen, Guangdong
2 4 6 8 10 9 7 5 3 1 (hardcover)
2 4 6 8 10 9 7 5 3 1 (reinforced)

All papers used by Bloomsbury Publishing, Inc., are natural, recyclable products made from wood grown in well-managed forests.
The manufacturing processes conform to the environmental regulations of the country of origin.

CHICK 'n' PUG
Meet
THE DUDE

Jennifer Sattler

BLOOMSBURY
NEW YORK   LONDON   NEW DELHI   SYDNEY

Chick and Pug were an unstoppable team.

They spent most of their time looking for exciting adventures and saving ordinary citizens.

But being a superhero can get tiring. Sometimes they just needed to relax, to kick back and play with some toys.

Then one day, after a long morning nap, they woke to find that their favorite toy of all, Squeaky Hamburger, was . . .

. . . missing!

Chick sprang into action. "You stay here
and keep a lookout while I investigate!"

"Whatever you say, little buddy," mumbled Pug.

Chick searched everywhere.

Pug just pointed.

"The Dude," he said drowsily.

Chick was hot on the Dude's tail,

but the Dude was a worthy opponent.

Chick's little legs were starting to get tired.

It looked like the rascal was about to get away when . . .

Pug saved the day, as only a Wonder Pug can!

(No dog can resist the nummy bone.)

Chick saw his chance. He snatched back Squeaky
Hamburger at last.

"Yuck."

"Now it's just a slimy, squishy hamburger." Chick sighed.

And he tossed it away.

"Don't worry, little buddy," Pug reassured his friend.

"Squeaky toys come and squeaky toys go."

"Oh, Pug! You're so wise!" gushed Chick.

"You're right. And we'll always have . . .

. . . each other."